JAPARRIKA RISES

PUFFIN BOOKS

UK | USA | Canada | Ireland | Australia
India | New Zealand | South Africa | China

Penguin Books is part of the Penguin Random House group of companies whose addresses can be found at global.penguinrandomhouse.com.

First published by Penguin Random House Australia Pty Ltd, 2018
This edition published by Penguin Random House Australia Pty Ltd, 2019

Text and illustrations by Tiwi College Alalinguwi Jarrakarlinga, with David Lawrence & Shelley Ware

Tiwi College Students
Tahleea Brogan, Shenaida Bush, Michaeline Mungatopi, Taylah Pati, Isobella Puruntatameri, Kimberley Stassi, Demaga Warrior

Printed and bound in Australia by Griffin Press, an accredited ISO AS/NZS 14001 Environmental Management Systems printer

ISBN 978 1 76 089464 1

A catalogue record for this book is available from the National Library of Australia

penguin.com.au

Penguin Random House Australia uses papers that are natural and recyclable products, made from wood grown in sustainable forests. The logging and manufacture processes are expected to conform to the environmental regulations of the country of origin.

ilf.org.au

Japarrika Rises

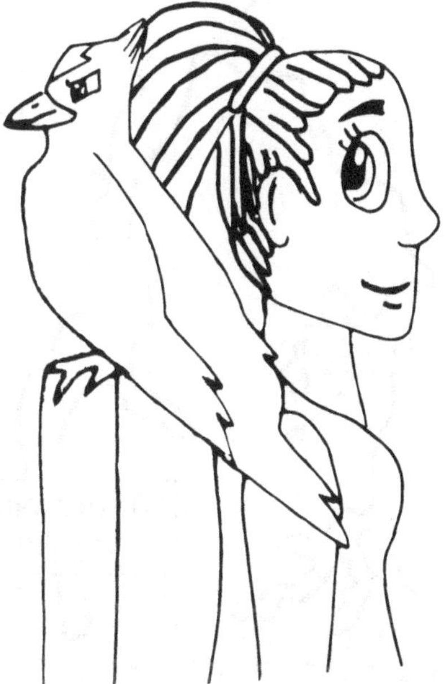

Written and illustrated by

TIWI COLLEGE
ALALINGUWI JARRAKARLINGA

With David Lawrence & Shelley Ware

PUFFIN BOOKS

TIWI ISLANDS

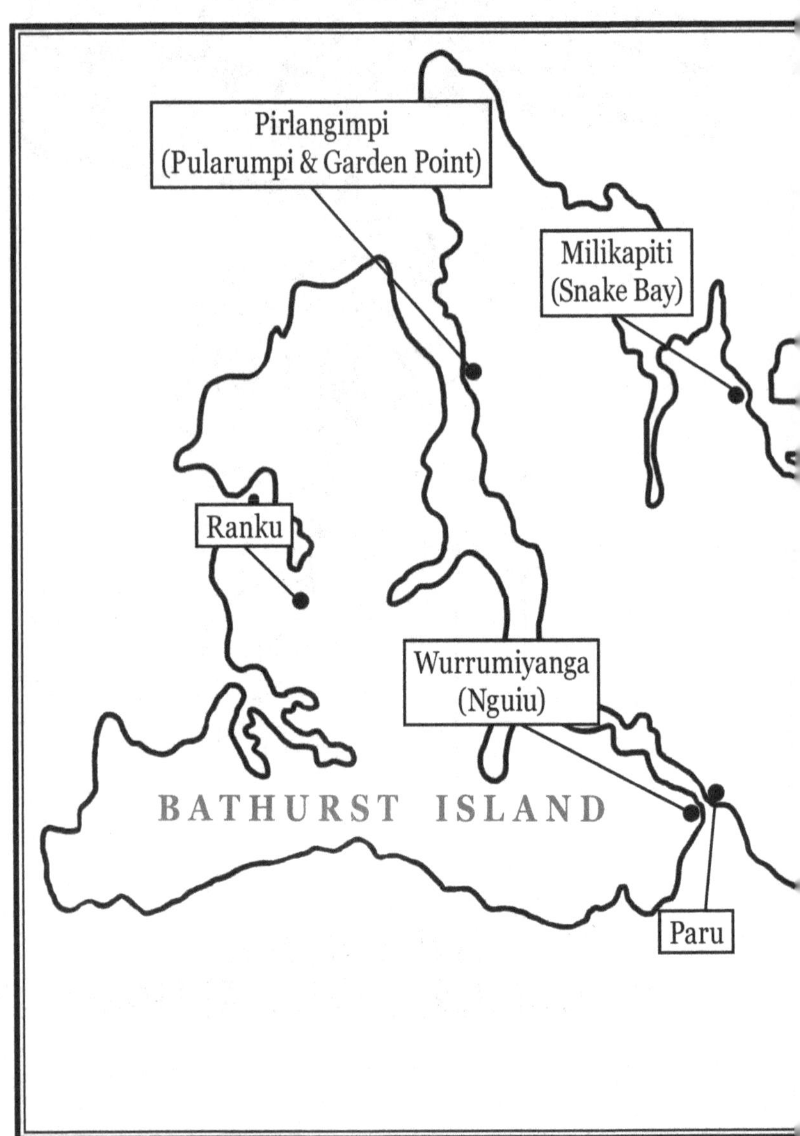

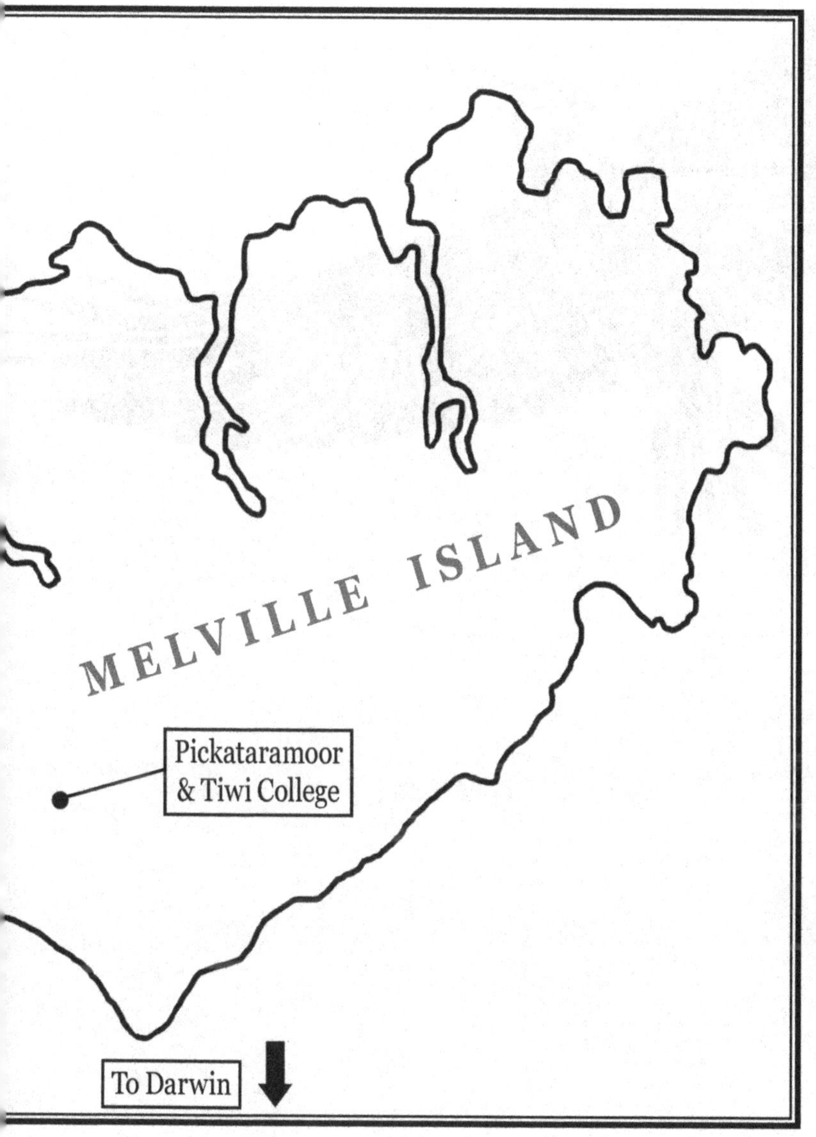
MELVILLE ISLAND
Pickataramoor
& Tiwi College
To Darwin

Japarrika is the Tiwi name for the Greater and Lesser Frigatebirds, which the Tiwi people call a storm bird. It lives on the shore or in the mangroves and when locals see it in the sky it tells them there's a storm coming.

'Japarrika' is also the name of the team song for the home side, the Tiwi Bombers, in the NT Football League.

1

Kay-Bell leaned on her mop and smiled. She was still thinking about the AFLW Lightning Series, which had been the best thing that ever happened to her.

She remembered kicking the winning goal of the game. And she remembered how her brother David called her *Japarrika* after the Storm Bird that followed her around. She had seen her parents in spirit, and the funniest part was seeing Aunty B being swooped by the plovers and them stealing her wig!

Kay-Bell really wanted to play in the Australian Football League Women's series, because she wanted to represent her family and culture.

That was her goal.

Suddenly her daydream was interrupted by a terrible sound. '*Aga!*' It was her mean Aunty's voice.

'Hey, stop daydreaming,' Aunty B said. 'What are you doing? Clean up!' Aunty B stared at Kay-Bell with her mean eyes.

'Wait, stop! What are you wearing? Give me that medal.'

Aunty B grabbed the golden medal that Kay-Bell had won in the Tiwi Warriors Lightning series, then she walked over to the front door, opened it and chucked the medal onto the roof. Aunty B rushed back towards Kay-Bell, and said, 'You're not going anywhere until you've finished cleaning, mopping the house down and cooking. You'll never make it through the NT Thunder squad and then get selected to go for the AFLW.'

Aunty B didn't support

Kay-Bell's dream of playing AFLW and that made it really hard for Kay-Bell to live her life. She wore a grumpy face.

'*Pwamika*,' Kay-Bell said under her breath as Aunty B turned her back.

But Aunty B stopped. 'What did you say to me?'

'I said "*pumpuka*",' Kay-Bell said, lying.

Aunty B didn't bother, she just kept on walking towards her couch to have a little *payi payi*.

'Kay-Bell,' yelled Aunty B, 'once you've done all of them other jobs, go and have a look at that magpie curry stew to see if it's cooked. Hurry up, I'm hungry. And get me some drinks from the fridge!'

2

The day had dragged on but there were only a few more jobs to finish. As Kay-Bell washed up she noticed the clock – it was almost time for footy training. She knew that Aunty B was in a deep sleep on the couch so without putting too much thought into the idea she grabbed her bag from under her bed and quickly snuck out of the house.

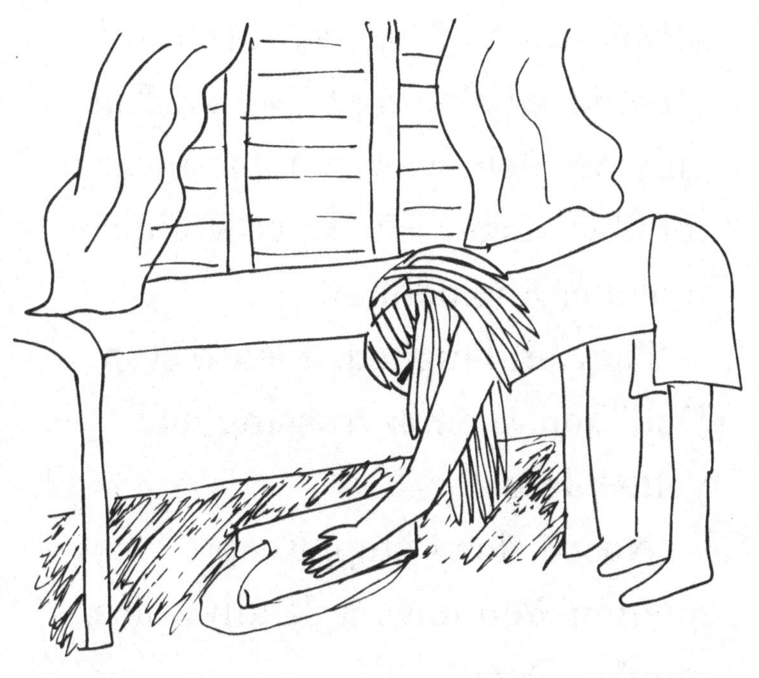

Every Thursday, Kay-Bell and her best friends, Jess and Dema, were driven to training by Jess's father, John, the local ranger. The car rides to training were always a lot of fun because they all enjoyed singing together. The only problem was that John was a terrible singer. His voice sounded like a crying donkey.

They all laughed. 'Please stop, Dad! You're embarrassing me!' yelled Jess.

'Noooo, don't stop. Keep singing! You have a deadly voice,' giggled Dema.

Footy training was great. They started with half an hour of fitness and then did half an hour of drills. They finished up with a scratch match, which all the girls loved.

Kay-Bell hoped that her aunty was still asleep on the couch and hadn't noticed she wasn't at home. As she was leaving training, Shane, the team's coach approached her.

'Congratulations, Kay-Bell!' he said.

'What are you talking about, coach?' asked Kay-Bell.

'You got selected to represent the NT. You put on a good show for them talent scouts at the Lightning Series.'

'Err what? Don't lie to me,' said Kay-Bell in shock.

Shane pulled out a piece of

paper from his pocket and showed it to Kay-Bell.

Kay-Bell, you have been selected to play for the NT Thunder under 18s team. Your flight leaves for Darwin at 9 am on Saturday and will return in the afternoon at 4 pm. Congratulations!

After reading the letter Kay-Bell screamed and danced in the middle of the oval. All the excitement that was running through Kay-Bell's body from the happy news made her forget that she had snuck out of the house so when she arrived home, she walked right through the front door.

Aunty B saw her and immediately snapped.

'Kay-Bell, where did you come back from? Did I say you could go out?'

'I went for a walk down the beach,' fibbed Kay-Bell.

'Then why are you in your footy gear? Don't lie!'

Kay-Bell rolled her eyes and walked towards her room while Aunty B continued to shout.

'And don't think you're going out anywhere on Saturday. I got lots of jobs for you to do,' she said.

Kay-Bell slammed the door with frustration.

She didn't know what to do. She had so many thoughts running through her head so she decided to call her brother up and ask him for help.

'Ahh, bro. I got picked for the Thunder team to play in Darwin on Saturday, but *Pwamika's* got me doing jobs all day.'

'Leave it with me, little sis. If you can get your friends to help out with the jobs, I'll take care of Aunty for the day.'

'How?' asked Kay-Bell.

'I'll take her out hunting.'

Kay-Bell looked out the window and saw a *japarrika* sitting on the fence. That's when she thought that this plan might just work.

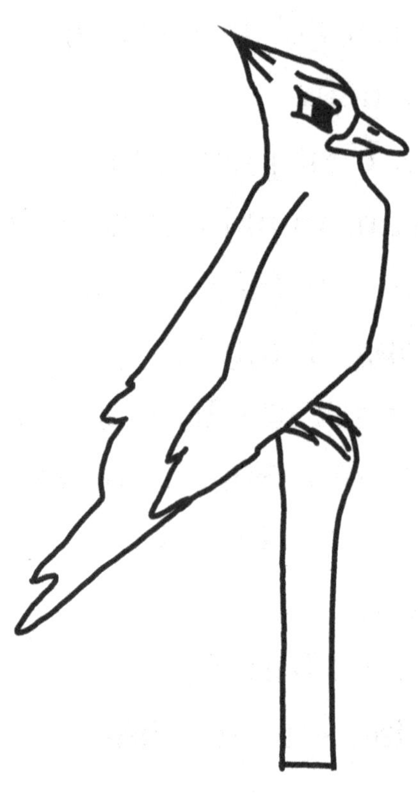

3

It was Saturday – game day! It was time for David's plan to be put into action. Everybody was ready to do their part to make sure Kay-Bell could get to Darwin to play for NT Thunder. This football carnival was very important to her because she really wanted to impress the NT Thunder coach, Rhiannon, and help her team win the games.

The moment had finally arrived. Kay-Bell was standing on the dirt road out the front of her house, waving goodbye to David and Aunty B. She was trying to look upset that she had to stay home and clean the house.

As the troopy drove away Aunty B put her head out the open window and yelled, 'Kay-Bell, clean the house!' She kept yelling it over and over, and the only thing that stopped her was when she nearly lost her favourite headscarf in the wind. Aunty B finally wound up the window and Kay-Bell just smiled and waved again.

'You can come out now, Dema and Jess,' whispered Kay-Bell.

Her friends stepped out from behind the mango tree, eating some mangoes.

'Don't worry about the jobs, Kay-Bell. We will clean the house. You just go and win that carnival.'

Kay-Bell ran inside and grabbed her footy bag and her lucky boots. Hugging Dema and Jess she said, 'Thank you. You guys are the best friends ever.'

David's wife, Kylie, beeped her car horn. She was out the front of

Aunty B's house to take Kay-Bell to the carnival. Kay-Bell jumped in the car and they headed to the airport to catch the charter plane to Darwin.

They arrived at the stadium just in time for the carnival so Kay-Bell ran straight into the change room and got into her footy gear.

'Good luck,' called Kylie.

Kay-Bell's enemy on the field, Sam, had made the NT Thunder team too. They'd often played against each over the past couple of years and they didn't like each other. Both of them were in the forward line, but neither of them were very happy about that. When Sam and Kay-Bell saw each other, they glared like two angry magpie geese.

Coach Rhiannon yelled out her final words to the team for game one. 'Good luck, girls! And make sure you help each other out there.'

The girls ran out to their positions. Kay-Bell was full forward and Sam ran into the forward pocket. The siren sounded, the crowd roared and it was game time.

Game one was a close one – goal for goal, fast and quick. It had heaps of high-flying specky marks and full body tackles that made the crowd go, 'Ooohhh'.

There were five minutes left in the second quarter when Sam got the ball, but she was too far out to kick a goal. Instead of kicking it to Kay-Bell, Sam ran towards the goals and bounced the ball. Kay-Bell should have shepherded but she didn't and Sam got tackled. They lost the ball and the other team kicked it to the opposite end and got a goal.

Rhiannon was really angry that her players hadn't worked as a team. She yelled out to the runner, 'Tell Kay-Bell to come off. I want to talk to her on the bench.'

Kay-Bell ran from the field, looking very worried. She knew that she'd done the wrong thing.

Rhiannon looked at Kay-Bell and said in an annoyed voice. 'You're off for the rest of the game, Kay-Bell. You didn't help your teammate out there and that's not what we're about.'

Kay-Bell was disappointed in herself. Maybe her dream of playing AFLW was over.

Kay-Bell couldn't believe that she was on the bench. Upset, she thought to herself, *Ahh, Sam's gonna make it to the AFLW and I'm not.*

Kay-Bell's legs were shaking and she scratched her head as she watched her team from the sideline. She thought about how she'd let down her brother and her friends. *Ahh, I'm so silly!*

I shouldn't worry about that murrutaka *Sam!! I should have played properly for the whole team.*

Sitting there, she watched as something happened on the field and her teammate was injured. Sam had gone for a tackle but before she got near her opponent, Sam grabbed the back of her leg and went red in the face. She looked like she was in lot of pain. Kay-Bell knew that Sam had pulled her hammy.

Rhiannon called over Kay-Bell. 'You're going on for Sam.'

Kay-Bell was so happy she

jumped up off the bench and started to stretch. When she ran on the field her heart was beating so fast and she told herself this was her time to shine.

But Kay-Bell also felt very nervous about this second chance. There was a lot of noise from the crowd and through all the yelling and cheers it was almost like she could hear her friends. She wished Jess and Dema were there to support her. But Kay-Bell suddenly realised that actually she didn't need her friends at this moment. *I got this one!*

Kay-Bell ran amok. She didn't stop running and did a couple of big tackles without dropping the ball once. She took a big specky on one of the opponents just on the fifty-metre line, and the crowd went wild as Kay-Bell lined up for a goal. She kicked a torpedo and it went straight through the middle of the four white poles.

'*Rhaaaaaaaaaa!*' went the crowd.

The siren went and Kay-Bell and her teammates were happy that they had won the game. Rhiannon told the girls to go and meet in the changing room. The team all walked across the field, chatting about the amazing win.

Kay-Bell and Sam were the last two to enter the change room. As they got to the doorway, Kay-Bell heard Sam whisper to one of the other players, 'Kay-Bell is a show off, hey. And she should go back to Tiwi where she comes from.'

But luckily Rhiannon heard it too and started to growl at Sam. 'Oi Sam, I heard that! That's some nasty words you said about Kay-Bell. I can't have you on my team if you say things like that about your teammate.'

Sam walked into the change room with her head down.

The team gathered around and Rhiannon stood against the wall with a piece of paper in her hand. Kay-Bell was so nervous her legs started to shake again. She knew that the team list for the NT Thunder trip to Canberra was on that paper. Rhiannon started to read out the names.

Kay-Bell thought that she wasn't going to make it because she'd been benched. If she didn't make the team trip, then her AFLW career might be over.

But the last name on the list was Kay-Bell's.

When Kay-Bell heard it she couldn't believe that she'd made the team. When the excitement had died down and Rhiannon's chat was over, she remembered that there was a big problem she still had to deal with.

OMG! I have to go back home before Aunty B comes back from hunting.

She quickly packed her stuff and they rushed to the airport.

5

Also that morning, David pulled away from Aunty B's house in his old troopy with its cracked windscreen. She yelled out the window at Kay-Bell until they were down the street.

'Come on, Aunty B. We got hunting to do. You ready?' he said.

Aunty B was sitting in the front passenger seat with her

scarf covering her bald head. As usual, she had her angry face on.

Aunty B said, 'What do you think, boy? I'm always ready to go hunting. You should know that. How many times you seen me being ready to go, you silly boy?'

They drove on a dusty red, bumpy road. After a few kilometres they went around a bend and David didn't see the big ditch ahead. When they hit it, Aunty B bounced up and down in the front seat like a big fat sloppy green frog. David looked at Aunty B, laughing at her. She turned to David with an even angrier face and exploded!

'David, you know how to drive, or what? I thought your father had been teaching you,' she yelled.

'Argh, Aunty B, you're too cheeky. Just relax. It was by

accident! I didn't see the ditch. And don't say that about my father not teaching me how to drive properly. My father is dead, he's gone, so have some respect,' David replied.

They argued all the way to the hunting spot. Normally Aunty B would call out to her ancestors to let them know they were there to hunt and to ask the spirits to look after them, but she was so busy arguing with David that she completely forgot.

When they arrived at their spot in the green trees, Aunty B got out of the troopy and thought to herself that she was going to get some good bush tucker today. She stepped into the slippery black mud and busted through the branches of the mangroves. She was looking for *jukwarringa* and *piranga* in between the mangrove roots. Aunty B's trick was rubbing her feet through the hot squishy mud to feel the sharp tip of the mud mussel shell. But Aunty B wasn't having any luck and she decided to yell out to David. 'Nephew, you found anything or what?'

'*Kurrukamini*, Aunty B. I can't find any *jukwarringa* anywhere, what's going on?'

They were both determined to find something and continued searching. Weaving through the tight spaces and squishy mud, they got tired and sweaty.

Aunty B found a pool of salt water to wash all the mud off her body and arms. She splashed some water on her face and suddenly realised from her reflection that her headscarf was missing. She looked up and saw *japarrika* had swooped down and stolen her pink silk scarf. It was sitting on a broken branch of the mangrove above. *Japarrika* flew off to another tree and Aunty B chased after it yelling, 'Bring back my scarf, you stinking bird!'

As she was running she tripped over a brown log and landed in the mud, her face was completely covered in smelly mud. When she stood up David looked at her and cracked up with a huge laugh.

'What are you looking at?' Aunty B yelled.

'Aunty B, I think you're prettier that way!' replied David with a cheeky smile.

Aunty B's face went bright red. 'What did you say, *bumbis*? You think I'm prettier this way? You wait! I'm gonna chase you with this big long stick!'

After chasing David for a while,

she said, 'Take me home now. I'm tired.'

'Well, only if you don't hit me with that big long stick,' David said.

Aunty B looked at David then threw away the stick and they walked back to the car together. When they jumped into the car David looked at his watch nervously. He hoped they wouldn't get back to the house before Kay-Bell did. Suddenly *japarrika* flew down and landed on the bonnet of the car. It seemed to give David a quick smile. He turned the key, but the car wouldn't start.

'Are you kidding me, David? What more can go wrong?' Then Aunty B realised what was going on. 'I know why we didn't have any luck today. It's because we didn't call out to our ancestors when we first arrived at the hunting spot.'

'That's because you were arguing so much with me, Aunty,' replied David.

'I wasn't arguing, you silly boy,' said Aunty B.

'Now you're arguing again!' laughed David.

'Just be quiet for a second. Help me to sing out to our ancestors,' said Aunty B.

Together they sang out. 'Oiiiiiiiiiiiiiiiii.'

And in the Tiwi way they

apologised to their ancestors and paid their respects.

'Try to start the car now,' said Aunty B.

David turned the key again and the car started straightaway.

Japarrika looked at both of them and flew up into the sky as the car took off.

They drove for a hundred metres, then all of a sudden Aunty B screamed, 'Stop the car, nephew! I think I saw something.'

Aunty B grabbed her gun and hopped out of the car. 'It's a young one *jarranga*.' Aunty B was a great shooter and took the buffalo down with only one shot.

'David, help me put this heavy buffalo in the back of the troopy. Quick, we need to get it home! Hurry!'

David looked down at his watch and hoped again that Kay-Bell had made it home.

6

Kay-Bell burst through the front door and luckily Aunty B wasn't home yet. Jess and Dema had done all the jobs for her while she was playing. She told them about the game and just as she was about to say what Sam got up to, they heard David's car pulling up out the front.

'Quick,' said Kay-Bell. 'You

gotta go before Aunty sees you!'

Jess and Dema jumped out the window just as Aunty B walked to the front door.

'Kay-Bell, where are you?' she yelled. 'Come here and help me with this *jarranga*!'

After preparing the meal they ate a tasty feast, and Kay-Bell was able to celebrate her football victory with the NT Thunder secretly. But how was she gonna convince Aunty B to let her go to Canberra?

***

The following Wednesday, David came back from hunting with a load of *nurringari*. He asked Kay-Bell if she could come over and help with the plucking.

His wife, Kylie, and their kids went over to Aunty B's place for a visit, so Aunty B didn't notice that Kay-Bell was gone.

David and Kay-Bell sat under a bushy tree, plucking the geese. It was a warm day, but luckily there was a cool breeze too, blowing the feathers all around them.

David explained to Kay-Bell that he had another plan. '*Abigo*, I was thinking we could go to Canberra to visit Kylie's family there. *Kuwa marri?* And while we're there you can play your NT Thunder game.'

Kay-Bell had been worrying

about how she would get to this game, so maybe this was the way!

But then she said, 'What if Aunty B asks you why I need to go with you mob?'

'It's okay, I'll tell her that I need you to come so that you can help me with the kids! She can't say no to that.'

Kay-Bell hoped he was right.

7

Without a doubt, Aunty B fell for it. Their plan had worked!

Kay-Bell felt relieved that she'd be able to play in Canberra.

That weekend, Jess and Dema waved goodbye to Kay-Bell, David, Kylie and their kids as they boarded the tiny charter plane to Darwin.

'Bye, Kay-Bell. We'll miss you,'

her friends both shouted.

As the plane took off Kay-Bell thought to herself, *I wish Dema and Jess could come to support me because Canberra is going to feel really far away from home.*

She hoped she could calm her nerves without them there.

As she leant her head on the plane window her niece cuddled up to her. They both closed their eyes and rested. After hours of travelling Kay-Bell and her family arrived in Canberra. They took her to the accommodation where the rest of her team was staying, so she could go straight to bed and have a good rest. Tomorrow was a big game.

***

There was so much energy running through Kay-Bell's body the next day before the game. As she sat in the change room she received a notification on her phone. Thinking it was a good luck message from Jess and Dema, she quickly checked it. But it was not a good luck message. Sam had posted an embarrassing photo of Kay-Bell on Facebook.

Her heart sank. Kay-Bell was sweating and her hands were shaking. For a moment she forgot about the game. All the preparation she'd done faded in a flash as she faced the post from Sam. She no longer felt ready to play her best for the AFLW scouts. Perhaps she wasn't good enough for the AFLW. Her nerves were as bad as they had ever been.

I can't do this, she thought.

'Kay-Bell, hurry up! We're about to run out onto the field,' shouted Rhiannon.

Kay-Bell could hear the

rest of the team getting pumped, ready to go. They were talking loudly.

'We got this! This is our time to shine.'

Kay-Bell wanted this so bad but couldn't face everyone after what Sam had done. A memory came to Kay-Bell. It was David's voice saying, 'From now on, we'll call you *Japarrika* – the Storm Bird.'

She was still shaking and feeling embarrassed, but David's words gave Kay-Bell some courage. She was *Japarrika*, she was the Storm Bird. She had come so far. If she didn't take the field, it would have all been for nothing, not to mention the growling she was likely to get from Aunty B when she found out why she really went to Canberra.

Kay-Bell checked her laces and took a deep breath.

'Kay-Bell, I'm serious. You need to get with the rest of the team,' yelled Rhiannon.

It was now or never. Kay-Bell rose to her feet and began walking to the door. As she got closer she broke into a run and caught up with her team. One of the players gave her a pat on the back as they jogged out on to the oval.

The siren blew loud, the girls were pumped and ready to play. They were there as a team but still all hoped to get the attention of the scouts. The first bounce took place and Kay-Bell didn't hesitate to take on the ball.

She scooped the ball up off the ground and booted it to one of her teammates, who took an amazing mark and scored a goal.

The cheering from the crowd was so loud that Kay-Bell couldn't even hear what they were saying. With all the adrenaline pounding through her veins she felt like she was *Japarrika*. She was no longer running; she was flying.

She could do this. She could even make it to AFLW.

But the game was close and it was goal for goal, so the hard work wasn't over yet.

By three-quarter time she wasn't holding back for anyone. Despite being a key forward she played the whole field. She was shepherding for her teammates, chasing her opponents down, not letting them score or have possession for too long.

But it didn't stop there. In the last quarter Kay-Bell was running the ball from the centre and kicking goals from inside the fifty-metre line. NT Thunder was in the lead by two goals, but now it was really time to impress the scouts.

In the dying seconds Kay-Bell took a huge screamer just outside the fifty-metre line. With a deep breath and slowly walking backwards, she lined up for goal and said to herself, 'This is for my mum and dad.'

She booted it straight through the middle just in time for the final siren.

8

Kay-Bell and her team were celebrating when she spotted her friends on the fence. Kay-Bell sprinted to where Jess and Dema were screaming out and jumping up and down. They both gave Kay-Bell a big hug and told her how they wanted to surprise her for her big game.

'Thanks for coming,' she said.

Kay-Bell then followed Rhiannon and the others to the change room, high-fiving each other. They were all exhausted and sweaty.

'That was an amazing game you played out there today.

I'm pretty sure the scouts were impressed with everyone's skills,' said Rhiannon. 'If you've been selected for the AFLW you will receive a letter in two days' time.'

Kay-Bell thought that this was her big chance to fulfil her dreams. She wanted it so much, but at the same time she was worried that her mean Aunty B might not let her go on to the next level of AFLW.

Kay-Bell stayed in Canberra with David and his family and they celebrated Kay-Bell's win. That night, David took Kay-Bell and her friends for a walk.

'You played well today, *abigo*. I know you'll get picked,' said David.

'But what if Aunty B doesn't let me play?' asked Kay-Bell.

'Don't worry about your baldy-headed aunty, you need to follow your dream,' laughed Dema.

David giggled quietly at the thought of his bald aunty.

Kay-Bell wasn't sure what to do. 'But who's going to look after me if I move away? Who's going to support me, and what about money?' she said.

'And who's going to look after Aunty B?' she asked.

David looked at his little sister and said, 'Don't worry, we'll figure it all out.'

'You watch,' said Jess. 'When we get back, you'll find that letter waiting for you.'

Kay-Bell was worried and excited at the same time. She knew it would be tough to move away from her normal life at home. On Tiwi there was hardly any traffic and it was quiet. The only things you heard back home were the wind blowing through the trees, plovers screeching while swooping at Aunty B, dingoes howling and horses trotting along the road. She knew if she moved, the weather would be different, and there would be too many buildings, too much traffic and at night she wouldn't be able to see the stars, like at home.

But at the same time she wanted to follow her dream.

***

The morning they left Canberra they all got up early. Kay-Bell was excited to go home and see if her letter had arrived. They jumped back on the big plane to Darwin, and then the little charter back home. David was driving slow on the road home, which made Kay-Bell frustrated.

'Can you speed up? I gotta get home before Aunty B sees my letter,' she said to David.

'Just relax, *abigo*. I can't drive fast 'cos the kids are in the car.

It's not safe,' said David.

Kay-Bell's legs were shaking again.

When she finally arrived home, she quickly jumped out of the troopy, grabbed her stuff and rushed into the house. She ran to the table, but saw no mail. There was nothing.

Her heart sank. She was devastated!

9

It had been three days since Kay-Bell's return from Canberra.

Every day she had asked her Aunty B, 'Hey, has any letter arrived for me?'

'No, no letter's come in yet. If there were any letters, I would've told you!'

This made Kay-Bell sad as she thought she hadn't made the team.

Aunty B turned around with a nasty face and she said, 'I know what you're up to! I know you have been sneaking around and playing footy. Well it looks like your footy career is over!'

Kay-Bell had had enough.

'I hate living in this house with you, *Pwamika*,' she said. 'You're just too lazy and grumpy! You make my life miserable, so I'm not living your dream any more. I'm chasing my own!'

Aunty B's face went so red it looked like lava.

But Kay-Bell kept talking. 'I'd rather stay with my big brother and his family,' she said. 'They are the only mob who cares about me. He encourages me and supports me every single day and he's always there for me.'

Aunty B completely cracked it and shouted, 'Kay-Bell, go to your room now!'

Aunty B quickly turned and walked towards her own bedroom. She took a deep breath to calm down and went over to her bed and sat down.

Suddenly there was a bright light next to her. It was Kay-Bell's mum who was visiting her in spirit.

Aunty B was shocked and scared.

'Now you know why I'm here,' said her sister. 'I put my trust in you to look after my daughter. I have watched you treating her like a slave, making her do all the jobs. I'm very disappointed in you. She's old enough to make her own choices. Not mine, not yours – Kay-Bell's choices! This will never happen again. Make sure you let her live her dream. My daughter is a good girl.'

Aunty B was terrified and could not move or speak. Then suddenly Kay-Bell's mum disappeared.

Aunty B got off the bed and walked towards the cupboard near the bedroom door. Grabbing a letter out of the drawer, she walked to Kay-Bell's room and knocked softly.

‘Can I come in?’ she asked.

Kay-Bell opened the door and saw Aunty B with tears in her eyes. She handed over an envelope and said, ‘I’m sorry. This letter arrived for you two days ago.’

As Kay-Bell opened the envelope *japarrika* landed beside the window and started singing. The letter was from the talent scout. They wanted her to play in the AFLW.

Kay-Bell burst into happy tears … her dream had finally come true.

GLOSSARY

abigo – little sister
aga – hey (when talking to a female)
bumbis – nephew
japarrika – Tiwi people call it a Storm Bird. It has a distinctive birdcall that lets people know rain and stormy weather is on its way.
jarranga – buffalo
jukwarringa – mud mussels
karrikamini – nothing

kuwa marri – yes, what do you think?
murrutaka – white girl
nurringari – geese
payi payi – sleep, nap
piranga – long bums
pumpuka – good
pwamika – death adder
troopy – a troop carrier, a large four wheel drive that carries up to 10 passengers

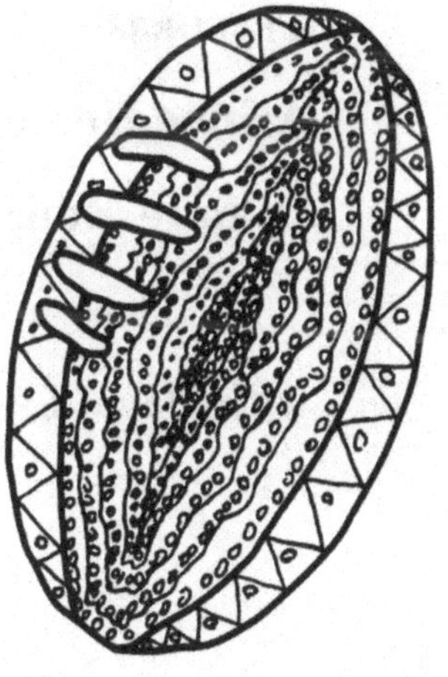

AUTHORS AND ILLUSTRATORS FROM TIWI COLLEGE

Students

Tahleea Brogan

Shenaida Bush

Michaeline Mungatopi

Taylah Pati

Isobella Puruntatameri

Kimberley Stassi

Demaga Warrior

Teachers

Ashlee Healey

Dianne Moore (Tictac)

with David Lawrence & Shelley Ware

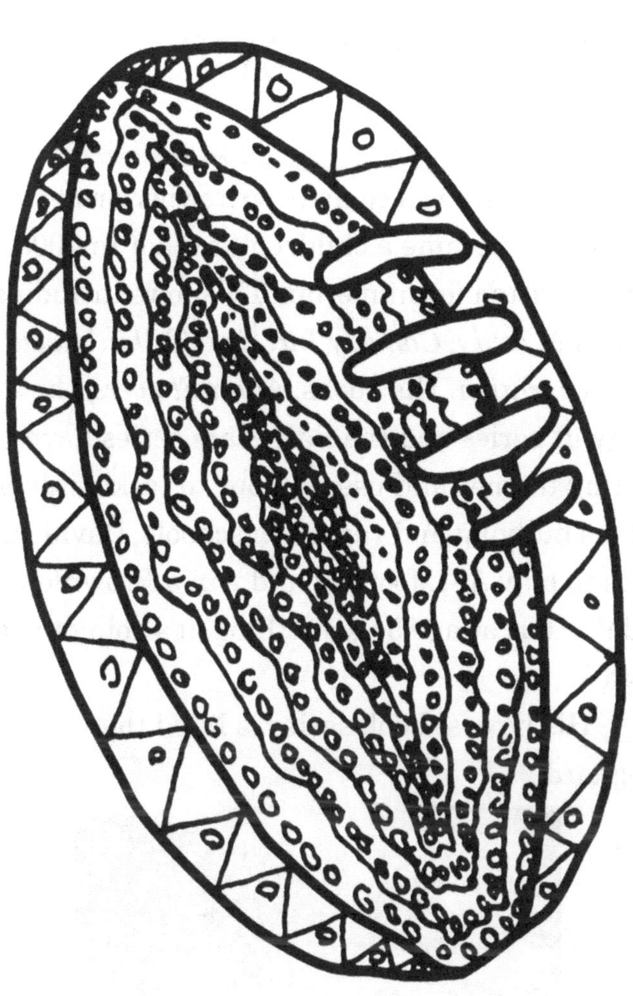

ABOUT DAVID

David Lawrence is a comedy writer/performer who accidentally became a children's author in 2008. He has written for numerous TV shows including *Hamish & Andy*, *Comedy Inc.*, and *Talkin' About Your Generation*. His books, *Anna Flowers,* the Fox Swift series and the Ball Stars series have sporting themes and use humour to tackle issues such as bullying and racism in schools. David still hopes to play AFL football and win a Brownlow Medal ... but at age 5o-something, it's going to be tough.

His newest book series is Maxi the Lifeguard.

ABOUT SHELLEY

Shelley Ware is a proud Yankunytjatjara and Wirangu woman from Adelaide, South Australia, who currently lives in Melbourne. She is well known as part of the ground breaking NITV football program *Marngrook*.

For the past decade or so, Shelley has worked in the media as a radio and television presenter on both local and national AFL football news shows. She has become one of the most respected and recognised female presenters of AFL football in the country.

Shelley also works part-time as a teacher at Kew Primary School in Melbourne where she is currently the Visual Arts teacher.

INDIGENOUS LITERACY FOUNDATION

Our vision is equity of opportunity. As a national book industry charity we aim to reduce the disadvantage experienced by children in remote Indigenous communities across Australia, by lifting literacy levels and instilling a lifelong love of reading. We do this through our three core programs: Book Supply, Book Buzz and Community Literacy Projects.

This book was produced as part of the ILF Create Initiative. This program partners young Indigenous women at Tiwi College with publishers and mentors to create (produce stories), cultivate (build knowledge) and motivate (grow self-esteem).

Find out more at ilf.org.au

CREATE INITIATIVE

Japarrika Rises was produced as part of the ILF Create Initiative. In November 2018, seven young Indigenous women from Tiwi College visited Sydney where, together with Penguin Random House staff and two mentors – David Lawrence and Shelley Ware – they created this book.

We thank everyone who helped to make this project happen.